WHILE THE WORLD IS SLEEPING

by Pamela Duncan Edwards   illustrated by Daniel Kirk

Orchard Books
New York

An Imprint of Scholastic Inc.

Come little sleepyhead, come with me,
I've left my hole high in the tree.

Oh, what wondrous things we'll see,
While the world is sleeping.

Climb aboard and hold on tight,
As I spread my wings in flight.

We will journey through the night,
While the world is sleeping.

Over rooftops we will sail,

Above the hills, across the vale,

Up toward the moon so pale,
While the world is sleeping.

In the meadow far below,
See father stag and mother doe.

Tiny fawns spring to and fro,
While the world is sleeping.

Silver fish are swimming past,

In the river running fast.

Will they reach the sea at last?

While the world is sleeping.

A bright-eyed fox is on the prowl,
He hopes to take a juicy fowl,

Until he hears the guard dog howl,
While the world is sleeping.

See baby rabbits as they play,
Round and round the bales of hay.

They'll have fun till light of day,
While the world is sleeping.

A beaver couple, fur agleam,
Work together as a team,

As they start their dam upstream,
While the world is sleeping.

In the woods, a porcupine,
Rattles quills to send a sign,

Don't come near, this food is mine!
While the world is sleeping.

A wise mouse mother squeaks, "Alarm!"
And tries to keep her babies calm.

No slithering snake must do them harm,
While the world is sleeping.

A sleek raccoon with bandit eyes,
Takes his nightly exercise.

In garbage cans he'll find his prize,
While the world is sleeping.

A lean, long-tailed and slinking rat,
Keeps an eye out for the cat.

A bat glides like an acrobat,
While the world is sleeping.

But now it's time to rest your head,
Safely tucked up in your bed,

As over earth the shadows spread,
While the world is sleeping.

For soon the rooster's song will warn,
Dark is gone, it's almost dawn.

The day is waiting to be born,
The world has finished sleeping.

Library of Congress Cataloging-in-Publication Data

Edwards, Pamela Duncan.

While the world is sleeping / Pamela Duncan Edwards ; [illustrations by] Daniel Kirk.–1st ed. p. cm.

Summary: A sleepy child is flown through the night sky to see foxes hunting, rabbits playing, raccoons scrounging, and other animals that are active while people sleep.

ISBN: 978-0-545-01756-5 (reinforced lib. bdg.)

[1. Nocturnal animals–Fiction. 2. Animals–Fiction. 3. Night–Fiction. 4. Bedtime–Fiction. 5. Stories in rhyme.] I. Kirk, Daniel, ill. II. Title. PZ8.3.E283Whi 2010 [E]–dc22 2007040283

10 9 8 7 6 5 4 3 2 1   10 11 12 13 14

Reinforced Binding for Library Use

First edition, January 2010

Printed in Mexico   49

The artwork was created using gouache on watercolor paper.

The book was set in NeutraText.